WHERE THE WILD THINGS ARE

WHERE THE WILD THINGS ARE

STORY AND PICTURES BY MAURICE SENDAK

PUFFIN BOOKS

in association with The Bodley Head

The night Max wore his wolf suit and made mischief of one kind

and another

his mother called him "WILD THING!"
and Max said "I'LL EAT YOU UP!"
so he was sent to bed without eating anything.

That very night in Max's room a forest grew

and grew—

and grew until his ceiling hung with vines
and the walls became the world all around

and an ocean tumbled by with a private boat for Max
and he sailed off through night and day

and in and out of weeks
and almost over a year
to where the wild things are.

And when he came to the place where the wild things are
they roared their terrible roars and gnashed their terrible teeth

and rolled their terrible eyes and showed their terrible claws

till Max said "BE STILL!"
and tamed them with the magic trick

of staring into all their yellow eyes without blinking once
and they were frightened and called him the most wild thing of all

and made him king of all wild things.

"And now," cried Max, "let the wild rumpus start!"

"Now stop!" Max said and sent the wild things off to bed
without their supper. And Max the king of all wild things was lonely
and wanted to be where someone loved him best of all.

Then all around from far away across the world
he smelled good things to eat
so he gave up being king of where the wild things are.

But the wild things cried, "Oh please don't go—
we'll eat you up—we love you so!"
And Max said, "No!"

The wild things roared their terrible roars and gnashed their terrible teeth
and rolled their terrible eyes and showed their terrible claws
but Max stepped into his private boat and waved good-bye

and sailed back over a year
and in and out of weeks
and through a day

and into the night of his very own room
where he found his supper waiting for him

and it was still hot.